SCOUT and ACE

Stuck on Planet Gloo

Written by Rose Impey
Illustrated by Ant Parker

ORCHARD BOOKS

Once upon a time, our heroes,

set out on a trip

into outer, outer-space.

Sucked through a worm-hole...

to a strange, new place,

lost in a galaxy called Fairy Tale Space.

The story continues...

Scout and Ace are in big trouble.

Their spaceship is losing power. It gets sucked onto the planet Gloo.

It lands with a bump.

On the planet lives
a giant called Glock.

When Scout and Ace see him . . .

. . . they race behind a rock.

Lucky for them Glock can't see,
but he can smell!

Scout and Ace look for a better place to hide.

They find a cave and creep inside.

But a voice says, "You can't hide in here. It's the giant's cave."

The cave starts to rumble and rock.

"Glock's coming!" Zack tells them. "Quick! Hide behind the clock."

Zack says, "No, Master. That smell must be these Mutants from Mars I've cooked for your tea."

Scout and Ace creep out from the clock,

but when Glock smells them

they hide in his sock.

The giant sniffs and he snuffs.
He huffs and he puffs.
Then he roars a loud roar.

Fee-Fi-Fo-Fog!
I know I can smell
a cat and a dog!

Zack says, "No, Master.
That smell must be the
Titan that's still in the trap.
Come along, now. It's time
for your nap."

When the giant's asleep,

Scout and Ace try again to creep out.

But the giant wakes . . .

. . . and starts to shout.

Fee-Fi-Fo-Four
-Five! I knew
I could smell
something alive!

Scout and Ace race out of the cave.

Glock races after them . . .

and Zack races after the giant.

Zack trips him up and the giant falls with a terrible . . .

The giant is dead.
Now Scout and Ace can leave.
And so can Zack.

This is one place they won't
be coming back to.

"Here's a joke," says Ace. "Two giants fell off a cliff. Boom! Boom! Think about it, Captain."

"Oh dear," groans Scout.
"Time we were going."

Fire the engines...

and lower the dome.

Once more our heroes...

are heading for home.

Enjoy all these stories about

SCOUT and ACE

and their adventures in Space!

Scout and Ace: Kippers for Supper
1 84362 172 X

Scout and Ace: Flying in a Frying Pan
1 84362 171 1

Scout and Ace: Stuck on Planet Gloo
1 84362 173 8

Scout and Ace: Kissing Frogs
1 84362 176 2

Scout and Ace: Talking Tables
1 84362 174 6

Scout and Ace: A Cat, a Rat and a Bat
1 84362 175 4

Scout and Ace: Three Heads to Feed
1 84362 177 0

Scout and Ace: The Scary Bear
1 84362 178 9

All priced at £4.99 each.

Colour Crunchies are available from all good bookshops, or can be ordered direct from the publisher:
Orchard Books, PO BOX 29, Douglas MM99 1BQ.
Credit card orders please telephone 01624 836000 or fax 01624 837033
or email: bookshop@enterprise.net for details.

To order please quote title, author and ISBN and your full name and address. Cheques and postal orders should be made payable to 'Bookpost plc'. Postage and packing is FREE within the UK – overseas customers should add £1.00 per book. Prices and availability are subject to change.

ORCHARD BOOKS, 96 Leonard Street, London EC2A 4XD.
Orchard Books Australia, 32/45-51 Huntley Street, Alexandria, NSW 2015.
This edition first published in Great Britain in hardback in 2004. First paperback publication 2005.
Text © Rose Impey 2004. Illustrations © Ant Parker 2004. The rights of Rose Impey to be identified as the author and Ant Parker to be identified as the illustrator have been asserted by them in accordance with the Copyright, Designs and Patents Act, 1988. A CIP catalogue record for this book is available from the British Library.
ISBN 1 84362 173 8   10 9 8 7 6 5 4 3 2
Printed in China